LAZY STORIES

W9-CKS-679

OTHER YEARLING BOOKS YOU WILL ENJOY:

The Thing at the Foot of the Bed and Scary Tales, MARIA LEACH

Jataka Tales—Fables from the Buddha, NANCY DEROIN, EDITOR

Beastly Boys and Ghastly Girls, WILLIAM COLE

The Witch's Egg, MADELEINE EDMONDSON

Once Under the Cherry Blossom Tree, ALLEN SAY

The Carp in the Bathtub, BARBARA COHEN

Nate the Great, MARJORIE WEINMAN SHARMAT

Morris Brookside, A Dog, MARJORIE WEINMAN SHARMAT

Flat Stanley, JEFF BROWN

Fiona's Bee, BEVERLY KELLER

YEARLING BOOKS are designed especially to entertain and enlighten young people. The finest available books for children have been selected under the direction of Charles F. Reasoner, Professor of Elementary Education, New York University.

For a complete listing of all Yearling titles, write to Education Sales Department, Dell Publishing Co., Inc. 1 Dag Hammarskjold Plaza, New York, N.Y. 10017

LAZY STORIES

Retold by Diane Wolkstein
Pictures by James Marshall

A YEARLING BOOK

Published by
Dell Publishing Co., Inc.
1 Dag Hammarskjold Plaza
New York, New York 10017

Text copyright © 1976 by Diane Wolkstein
Pictures copyright © 1976 by James Marshall

Yearling ® TM 913705, Dell Publishing Co., Inc.

ISBN: 0-440-44643-0

Reprinted by arrangement with The Seabury Press.
Printed in the United States of America
First Yearling printing—November 1977

CW

For Benny Zucker: the Sweetest Lazy

Contents

Hiroko

Japanese children are very good and always do what they are told. As soon as they can talk, they are taught to keep their room clean and never to dirty the mat.

The Japanese walk, sleep, eat, and write on the mats, so they must be kept perfectly clean. And the Japanese fairies, who live in the mats, frighten careless children who drop anything on the mats or dirty them in any way.

Now tell me, do you really think *all* Japanese children are that good? Aren't there any mischievous or lazy ones? Well yes, there are, and this is a story about one of them: a Japanese girl named Hiroko.

Hiroko's parents were so rich that Hiroko had three servants of her own. She never had to do anything, for her servants did everything for her. In the morning Hiroko had only to cough slightly, *heh-heh*, and immediately her servants were at her bedside. They undressed her and washed her and dressed her. *Heh-heh*. They brushed and combed her hair and arranged it just so. Hiroko grew up without ever having learned to wash her own hands.

When Hiroko was a young woman, a brave samurai fell in love with her and asked her parents if he might marry her. Although he was not a wealthy man, he had such a fine reputation for courage in battle that Hiroko's parents agreed.

Hiroko went to live at the samurai's house. He was too poor to have any servants, so Hiroko, who had never even learned to wash her own hands, had to learn to cook and clean and sew. It really wasn't *that* much to do. But as Hiroko had never before done any work, at the end of the day she could scarcely wait to lie down. She never even bothered to put away the toothpicks with which she cleaned her teeth, but simply let them drop down beside her into the mat.

One night when her husband was away, Hiroko was awakened at two o'clock in the morning, the hour of the ox, by a strange noise:

By the light of the lamp she could see hundreds of little men, not more than an inch high, rising out of the mat and marching toward her. They were dressed as samurai warriors and each of them carried a sword and wore his hair in a knot at the top of his head. The little men marched right up onto her covers, and sang in high piercing tones:

> *"Chin-chin, Kobakama, Yomo fuké soro"*
> *"Chin-chin, Kobakama, Yomo fuké soro"*

The words were nice enough. They meant: "We are the Chin-Chin, the Kobakama. The hour is late, the night is falling." But the expressions on the men's faces were cruel and mocking.

"Chin-chin, Kobakama, Yomo fuké sōro"
"Chin-chin, Kobakama, Yomo fuké sōro"
"Chin-chin, Kobakama, Yomo fuké sōro"

They were making fun of her. She pushed them off her covers, but they bounced up again. She pushed them away a second time, but again they bounced back.

"Chin-chin, Kobakama, Yomo fuké sōro!"
"Chin-chin, Kobakama, Yomo fuké sōro!"

All night they danced about her pillow and only in the morning did they disappear.

Hiroko was ashamed to tell anybody what had happened, for she was the wife of a brave samurai warrior and she did not want anybody to know how frightened she had been.

The next night, at the same time, the little men reappeared.

"Chin-chin, Kobakama, Yomo fuké soro!"
"Chin-chin, Kobakama, Yomo fuké soro!"

Every night they came and danced about her pillow. Hiroko grew more and more tired and weak until finally she became sick and her husband was sent for.

"My darling," he said in the gentlest voice. "What has happened to you?"

At first Hiroko did not want to tell him, but as he spoke so kindly and looked so worried, she finally did.

"How is it possible?" he said. "Tiny warriors an inch high?" And he laughed. But when he saw his wife's earnest and frightened face, he knew that for her they existed. "Do not worry," he assured her. "Tonight I shall hide in the closet and I will be ready for them."

That night Hiroko went to bed and her husband waited in the closet. At two o'clock, the hour of the ox, the little men rose from the mat and marched toward Hiroko's bed.

"Who could they be" thought the samurai, "dancing about with such cruel expressions on their faces?" Then the samurai knew. "The mat fairies!" he cried. And he rushed out of the closet

swinging his sword at them.

The little men fell to the floor in a heap. What were they? They were . . . toothpicks!

Night after night, that lazy woman had dropped her toothpicks into the mat. To the fairies who lived in the mat it sounded like thunder. Night after night, their sleep had been disturbed.

Finally the fairies had had enough. They crept into the toothpicks and transformed them into samurai warriors to frighten the woman out of the house.

"Toothpicks!" said the husband. He picked them up and burnt them. And the fairies slipped back into the mat. "Where could so many toothpicks have come from?" he asked.

17

Hiroko did not answer, but she took care never to drop another toothpick, or anything else, into the mat. For the fairies sleep there, and they need their peace and quiet, too.

The Tatema

At six o'clock in the morning Mario was fast asleep. And he was still asleep at seven, at eight, at nine, at ten. Usually Mario would wake up about eleven. Then he would ask his wife to go to the store to get tortillas and coffee for his breakfast.

Fortunately for Mario, the storekeeper was a childhood friend of his and never asked him to pay for his food. But one morning the storekeeper woke and said to himself: "Why should I work so hard, getting up at five every morning, while my friend lies in bed all day enjoying himself? No. He will have to help me before I give him any more food."

That morning when Mario's wife arrived at

the store, the storekeeper refused to give her any food. "Tell your husband that I'm building an extra room on my house and I want him to help me carry some large rocks from the quarry. After he helps me, then you can come for the food."

"Oh no!" said Mario, when he heard what the storekeeper had said. "Those rocks are much too heavy for me to move. How many times must I say: If God wishes to give, He will give, even if He has to push it in through the window? Please, no more talk of work." With that, he dressed and left the house.

Mario was walking up the hill and watching the clouds drift across the sky, when suddenly he heard shouts behind him.

"Whoa! WHOO-AA!"

Turning around, he saw a runaway horse, heedless of his rider's cries, charging up the path.

"WHOO-AA WHOA!" the rider cried again, but the horse paid no attention.

Just as the animal raced by, Mario leaped forward without thought for himself, grabbed the bit, and brought the horse to a halt.

Mario held the reins while the rider dismounted. The rider was an old man with a long white beard.

"You are both wise and brave," he said to

Mario. "You do not run here and there like the others, but when the moment is important, then you are there. You risked your life for me today and I want to reward you by giving you a tatema."

Mario looked puzzled.

"A tatema is a gift given by God to man," the old gentleman explained, "and only the man God gives it to may keep it."

He motioned for Mario to follow him and they continued up the hill. Then the gentleman stopped and pointed to a large flat rock. "Underneath that rock," he said, "are oak leaves. Under the oak leaves are wooden chests. If you open the chests you will find the tatema waiting for you."

Mario bent down and pushed aside the rock. He brushed aside the leaves, and there were six wooden chests. Slowly he opened one of the chests.

It was filled with silver coins. He opened a second chest. It too was filled with silver coins. He opened a third . . . all six chests were filled with silver! Mario turned around to thank the old gentleman, but he and his horse were gone.

Mario scooped up a handful of coins and put them in his pocket. Then he closed all six chests, covered them with leaves, and put back the rock. By now he was exhausted. He sat down under a tree to rest and fell asleep.

When Mario woke up, it was late in the afternoon and he was hungry. As he hurried down the hill for his supper he heard a clinking noise. He stopped. The noise stopped. He started on again and the clinking began again. Then he put his hand in his pocket and brought out . . . six silver coins.

When Mario's wife put the coins in the storekeeper's hands, she said: "My husband sends you these. We need rice, beans, a chicken, tortillas, tomatoes, and coffee."

The storekeeper looked at the silver coins in amazement. "How did Mario get so much money?" he wondered aloud.

"Come to our house tomorrow," the wife said, "and he will tell you."

The next afternoon the storekeeper heard the whole story.

"But, Mario," he asked, "why didn't you bring the chests home with you?"

"Oh, they were much too heavy," Mario said. "I would need mules to carry them and I have no mules. Anyway, by now, dear friend, you should know: If God wishes to give, He will give, even if He has to push it in through the window."

"*I* have mules," the storekeeper said. "I will come to your house tonight and we will go to the rock together. If you give me three of the chests, my mules will carry all six down the hill. What do you say?"

"Fine," said Mario

The storekeeper returned to his store. But the whole rest of the day he kept thinking to himself: "Why should I divide the treasure with Mario? After all, it is I who own the mules. He will never own mules. He would never even know what to do with his share of the money. Whereas I, I shall buy more mules, build a larger house . . ."

That night at eleven o'clock Mario was sound asleep.

"Husband," said his wife. "Wake up. It is past eleven and your friend has not come."

"Oh, he's just late," said Mario and he fell back asleep.

An hour later the wife woke her husband again.

"Husband, wake up! It's midnight and I'm afraid your friend has decided to keep all the silver for himself."

"Midnight? So late? It's much too late to go anywhere now. Wife, come to sleep."

So the wife lay down and she and Mario both slept soundly through the night.

Meanwhile the storekeeper had arrived at the flat rock with his mules and his servants. He ordered the servants to remove the rock and look

under the leaves. They did so and found the six wooden chests. "Open them quickly!" the storekeeper said. But when the servants opened them, they saw the chests were filled, not with silver, but with foul-smelling mud.

"My friend has tricked me!" the storekeeper cried. "Well, I will trick him right back!" He ordered his servants to load the chests onto the mules, to carry them down the hill, and to dump all the mud in front of Mario's house. They did this and rode away.

The next morning when Mario's wife woke up, she could not open the door. She tried the wooden window, but it too was stuck.

"Husband, wake up," she said. "There is something outside our house and we are trapped inside."

Mario got out of bed, and he pushed on the window while she pushed on the door. Then he pushed on the door while she pushed on the window. She pushed and pushed and pushed, and at last the window opened a crack. A shower of silver coins fell onto the floor.

"Husband," the wife said, "your friend came after all!"

Later that morning the wife went to the store and ordered not only food, but new clothes for herself and Mario. Before the storekeeper could question her, she put down on the counter twenty silver coins and said:

"How kind you have been to us! We waited last night until midnight and I was afraid you had changed your mind. But then this morning the coins came pouring in through the window. Surely you gave us more than half."

"No, no," the storekeeper protested. "It wasn't me."

"Of course it was you. Who else would have left all those silver coins outside our house?"

There was silence in the store.

Then the storekeeper said quietly, "Your husband has already told us: If God wishes to give, He will give . . . even if He has to push it in through the window."

The Fig-Tree Beggar
and the Willful Princess

There was once a boy named Khotan, who was very lazy. He was so lazy he refused to feed himself. He would open his mouth wide and wait until his mother cut his food into small pieces. Then he would chew the pieces slowly and smile happily. He did this until he was seventeen years old!

When Khotan was seventeen, his mother died. The villagers thought that now Khotan would surely find work and begin to feed himself. But no. Khotan just walked into the forest, lay down under a fig tree, opened his mouth wide, and waited until the ripe figs fell off the tree and into his mouth.

One morning a man from another village was

passing through the forest and heard cries for help. "H-e-l-p! I'm starving. I'm dying. H-e-l-p." He ran quickly toward the cries and saw a young man stretched out on his back under a sweet fig tree, calling: "H-e-l-p!"

As the man knelt down to see if the boy were ill, Khotan smiled up at him and said: "Be so kind as to shake the branches of the fig tree. The wind has stopped blowing and I haven't had one fig all day."

"You lazy good-for-nothing!" the man said, and shook the tree in anger, scattering figs in all directions. Then he turned and stomped off.

Khotan jumped up. He grabbed a handful of figs and threw them at the man. They missed him and fell into the river. The man did not return, so Khotan lay down again under his tree.

The figs floated slowly downstream until, in the late afternoon, they came to the place where Chaidiao, the Princess of the province, was bathing. She saw them and reached out and tasted one. It was delicious. She tried another. It too was delicious. There was one more, and she ate that.

Then she told her father, the Chow, about the figs and asked for more of the same. But none quite like them could be found. Yet Chaidiao could not forget their taste. She looked for them during the day and dreamed of them at night. Finally she told her father she would marry the man who would bring her those figs. She would marry him and none other.

"What nonsense!" her father said. "What willfulness!" But the Princess talked so incessantly about the figs, that at last the Chow declared that all the men of the province should appear at the meeting hall.

When they gathered in the meeting hall, the Chow announced:

"The Princess has promised to marry the man who will bring her a certain fruit. Are all the men of the province present?"

"No. Khotan would not come," someone called out. "He said he cannot leave his tree."

"Then carry him!" the Chow ordered. "Every man must be present."

The Chow's servants went to speak with Khotan. They offered to carry him, but he refused

to abandon his tree. Only when they promised to pick him a good supply of figs to take with him, did he agree to being carried to the palace.

"Khotan, the fig-tree beggar!" the servants announced when they arrived at the meeting hall.

The Chow looked in horror at Khotan. Not because Khotan was dressed in rags, his face streaked with dirt, his hair caked with mud, but because of what he carried in his arms: FIGS. And the very ones the Princess had described.

"Daughter," the Chow asked, "are the figs in this man's lap the figs you have been looking for?"

"Yes, father," she answered happily. "Yes, these are my figs!"

"Then prepare for your wedding, my willful daughter, for your husband has arrived!"

Khotan and Chaidiao were married the next day by a Buddhist monk.

The Chow was so angry that his daughter had chosen such a husband, he banished them both from the province. They were placed in a barge without oars and left to drift down the river toward the open sea.

Khotan remained in the position in which he had been placed, staring with a wide happy grin at his beautiful bride. Chaidiao stared fearfully back at him, wondering what would happen.

But nothing happened. Khotan just sat there.
The day passed and then the night. Khotan
did not move. The next morning Chaidiao was
hungry and restless. Now she hoped Khotan
would do something. But no. He just sat there.

On the second evening the barge got stuck in
the mud along the shore. Chaidiao sat up expec-
tantly, waiting for Khotan to speak, to move, to
look for food. No. Khotan just sat where he was.

The next morning when Khotan woke up,
Chaidiao was gone. Suddenly Khotan was hun-
gry, very hungry. And where was his wife?
Where was Chaidiao?

Khotan went into the forest to find her, and
came to a Buddhist monastery. The monks gave
him rice and rice seedlings, and he brought them

back to the barge. But the Princess had not returned.

Khotan set the seedlings in the shade and sat down to eat the rice. Without thinking he finished all the rice, then he realized: When Chaidiao returns, *if* Chaidiao returns, what will she eat?

It was almost dark when Chaidiao came out of the forest, her arms filled with fruits and wild berries. She went to the barge but Khotan was not there. She began to look for him along the river's edge and saw him bending over a row of rice seedlings he had just planted.

So they began to live together. Khotan worked in the rice fields and Chaidiao gathered fruit and tended their garden. In the evening they slept near the barge.

After many months the gods above noticed Khotan, the once lazy beggar, working hour after hour in the hot rice fields. They decided to reward him, and in the midst of a dreadful thunderstorm, they forged a bronze gong and gave it to the lightning to carry down to the earth.

The next morning Khotan found the beautiful gong lying in the middle of the rice fields. "I shall give it to Chaidiao as a present," he thought, and he struck it once to hear its sound.

Immediately the rags he was wearing fell from him and he was dressed in silk clothes. He struck it a second time: he became tall and straight. A third time: his face shone with beauty. A fourth time: servants surrounded him, kneeling before him. A fifth time: musicians joined them. And the sixth time: wisdom entered his heart.

Khotan then returned to the boat surrounded by the servants and musicians. Chaidiao, thinking he was some great foreign prince, bowed her head to the ground.

"Great one! Honored one!" she said. "How may I serve you?"

"Food!" he answered.

Chaidiao prepared rice and fruit and served the prince. But when he insisted that she cut up his food into tiny pieces, she looked at him more closely. She looked right into his eyes.

"Khotan?" she whispered.

And the great foreign prince smiled, and, looking into her eyes, whispered back: "Chaidiao?"

Then Khotan designed a magnificent wooden ship, and while his servants built it, his musicians played for him and Chaidiao.

Soon news of the foreign prince reached the province of the Chow, and the Chow sent an invitation to the prince, asking him and all his royal retinue to the palace.

The Chow went down to the river to greet the royal party. And when he saw his own daughter walking off the ship at the side of the foreign prince, he could not stop himself from crying out in astonishment: "CHAIDIAO!"

"Yes, father," she answered. "You invited us, and we have returned."

So it was that Khotan and Chaidiao came to
live again in the province of the Chow. And when
the Chow died, Khotan, the fig-tree beggar, became Chow. He was considered a wise and gen-
erous ruler by all. And he was. Except . . . he
had one peculiarity that no one understood: he
refused all invitations to dinner and never ate
in public.

Why? Well, he much preferred to stretch out
on the floor of his bedroom while his wife cut his

food into tiny pieces and dropped them into his
mouth . . . one by one.

A Storyteller's Notes

For me the most fun in storytelling comes when, knowing a story inside out, I suddenly realize something I never understood before. It could be tasting just how very good that fig did taste, or hearing the sweetness of the moment of silence at the end of *Hiroko.*

I come to these discoveries from my own understanding and from watching my listeners. One licked her lips as I tasted the first fig. Another nodded his head up and down, up and down, at the words, "they need their peace and quiet, too." When you tell the stories, you will make your own discoveries. If you are willing, write and share some of them with me.

Hiroko

Hiroko is one of those rare stories that can be told at almost any social gathering and will delight audiences of all ages. I have told it at nursery schools and day care centers, at elementary school assemblies, at senior citizen centers, and in the parks to the young, ages four to eighty-four.

The fear of being unprepared for what is expected of you is shared by all ages, and the mystery of the miniature men rising out of the mat fascinates every curious imagination.

Sometimes young children, four to seven years, enjoy learning and repeating with me the Japanese words. I chant both the "strange noise" and the Japanese words in a high, shrill, nasal voice to make them seem unearthly. Approximately seven minutes telling time. Two minutes reading time.

The Tatema

The Tatema almost tells itself, for it is constant adventure and intrigue. But be assured of one thing: Mario, though he is an innocent, is no fool. He is the one who, because of his complete and unshakeable faith in God's ways, rescues the stranger and saves himself and his wife.

The first time Mario says the phrase, If God wishes to give, He will give, even if He has to push it in through the window, it should be spoken rather quickly and off-handedly. It is common knowledge between himself and his wife. The second time Mario says it, it should be slower, for Mario is forced to explain it once again to his rather bull-headed and earthy friend. The third time the phrase is spoken, it should be said slowly and haltingly, for the speaker has understood the meaning for the first time.

It is better to tell this story to children six years old and up. Younger children do not fully understand the silver-mud transformation. I found it especially effective with slow readers in fourth, fifth, and sixth grades. Approximately nine minutes telling time.

The Fig-Tree Beggar and the Willful Princess

The audience, regardless of age, is snatched up in the first paragraph. What perversity, obstinacy, and sheer luxury to be so pampered! And yet, what irony that Khotan, who has been so improperly nurtured and spoiled, is brought together with Chaidiao, the Princess, because they both hold in common the most indomitable of wills.

I often personalize the boy's stubbornness, depending on the ages of my listeners, i.e., "when he was four years old, he did this, *and* when he was five years old, *and* when he was *seven* years old. . . ."

I smack my lips and taste the inside of both cheeks with relish as Chaidiao tastes each fig—this helps to concretize and explain Chaidiao's fruit-passion.

I strike my hands together (like cymbals) on each successive stroke of the gong. I hold my hands pressed against each other until I've described each transformation. Then I strike anew, building with each clap, and not pausing in the recounting, until the sixth and last clap, so that the magic will not be broken. The clap, if done with such an intention, can be likened to bringing heaven and earth together, which is the moment when miracles may happen.

This story works well with audiences of mixed ages, four years and up. Each age understands and enjoys the story differently. The different levels of enjoyment—the younger children laugh at different parts than the older—add to the vitality and strength of the story. The story is especially effective with children seven to ten years old. Approximately eleven minutes telling time.

Khotan (pronounced ′Kō-tan) means "beggar" in Laotian. Chaidiao (pronounced Chī-dio) means "one heart."